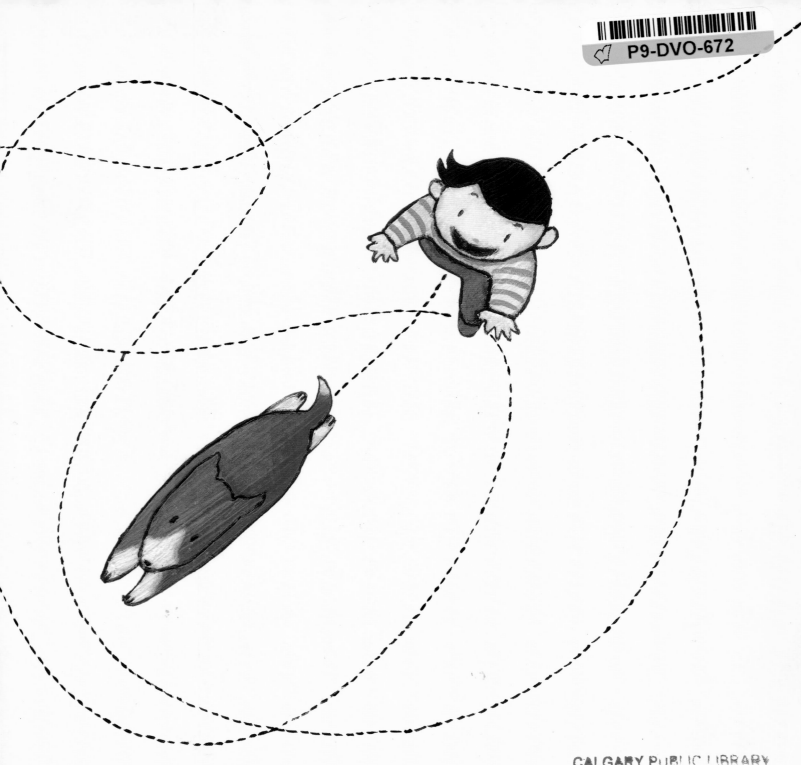

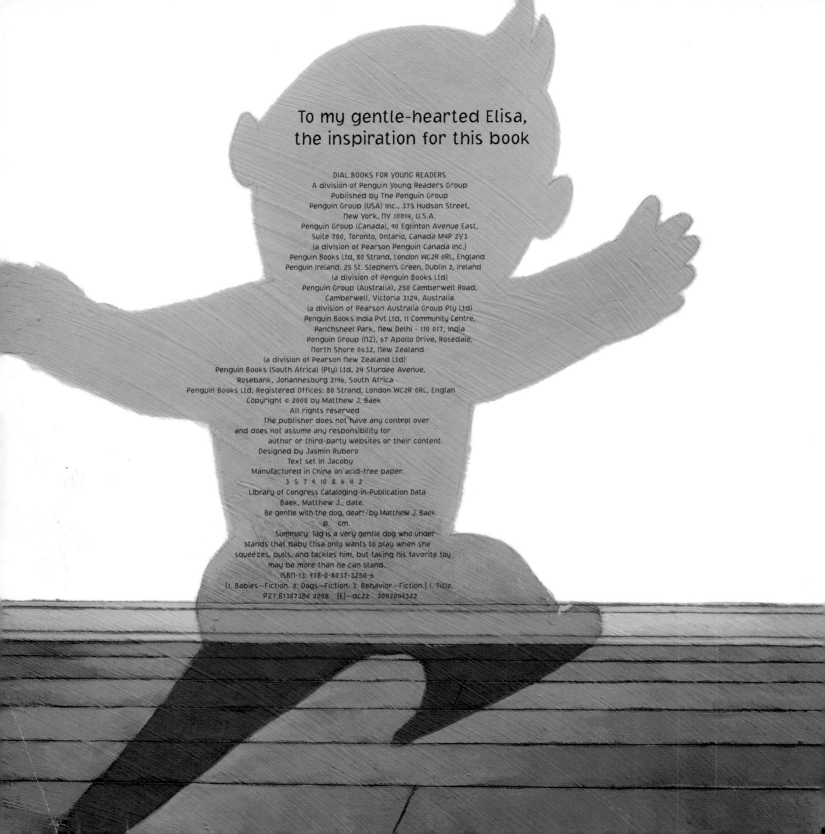

**To my gentle-hearted Elisa,
the inspiration for this book**

DIAL BOOKS FOR YOUNG READERS
A division of Penguin Young Readers Group
Published by The Penguin Group
Penguin Group (USA) Inc., 375 Hudson Street,
New York, NY 10014, U.S.A.
Penguin Group (Canada), 90 Eglinton Avenue East,
Suite 700, Toronto, Ontario, Canada M4P 2Y3
(a division of Pearson Penguin Canada Inc.)
Penguin Books Ltd, 80 Strand, London WC2R 0RL, England
Penguin Ireland, 25 St. Stephen's Green, Dublin 2, Ireland
(a division of Penguin Books Ltd)
Penguin Group (Australia), 250 Camberwell Road,
Camberwell, Victoria 3124, Australia
(a division of Pearson Australia Group Pty Ltd)
Penguin Books India Pvt Ltd, 11 Community Centre,
Panchsheel Park, New Delhi - 110 017, India
Penguin Group (NZ), 67 Apollo Drive, Rosedale,
North Shore 0632, New Zealand
(a division of Pearson New Zealand Ltd)
Penguin Books (South Africa) (Pty) Ltd, 24 Sturdee Avenue,
Rosebank, Johannesburg 2196, South Africa
Penguin Books Ltd, Registered Offices: 80 Strand, London WC2R 0RL, England

Designed by Jasmin Rubero
Text set in Jacoby
Manufactured in China on acid-free paper
3 5 7 9 10 8 6 4 2
Library of Congress Cataloging-in-Publication Data
Baek, Matthew J., date.
Be gentle with the dog, dear! / by Matthew J. Baek.
p.   cm.
Summary: Tag is a very gentle dog who under-
stands that baby Elisa only wants to play when she
squeezes, pulls, and tackles him, but taking his favorite toy
may be more than he can stand.
ISBN-13: 978-0-8037-3250-6
[1. Babies—Fiction. 2. Dogs—Fiction. 3. Behavior—Fiction.] I. Title.
PZ7.B13873Be 2008   [E]—dc22   2007004322

Be Gentle with the Dog, Dear!

Matthew J. Baek

Dial Books for Young Readers

This is Tag. He's a lap dog, a gentle dog.

Matt and Jin
are his owners.
They love him, and
he loves them back.

Then there's Elisa, their daughter.
She's a precious baby . . .

when she's sleeping.

Other times she's not so precious.

Like when . . .

she squeezes Tag,

and pulls his tail,

and tackles him.

He knows it's her way of showing love,
but the truth is . . .

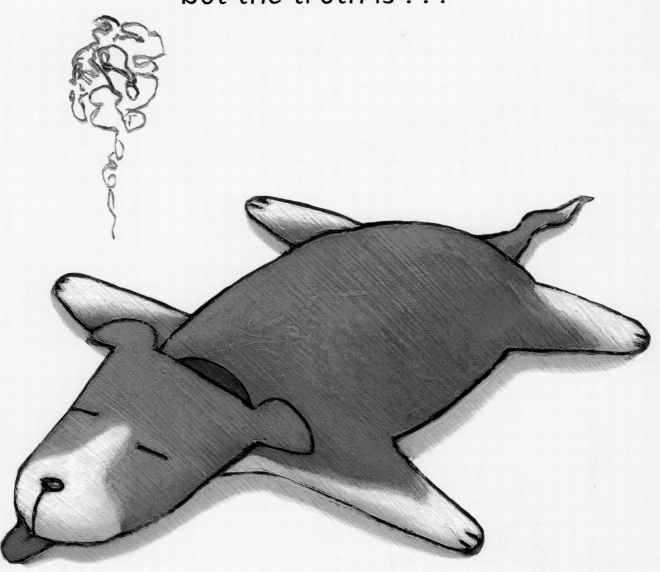

he's miserable.

Jin and Matt tell Elisa,
"Be gentle with the
dog, dear."

But soon enough, she is at it again.

There she is . . .

and here she comes!

Once again,

she squeezes him,

she pulls his tail,

and she tackles him.

And then . . .

she takes his toy.
His *favorite* toy.

GRRRrrrrr

That's it. Tag can't take it anymore.

Oh, rats.

"Elisa, you *must* be gentle
with the dog, dear."

Uh–oh.

She *is* a precious baby.

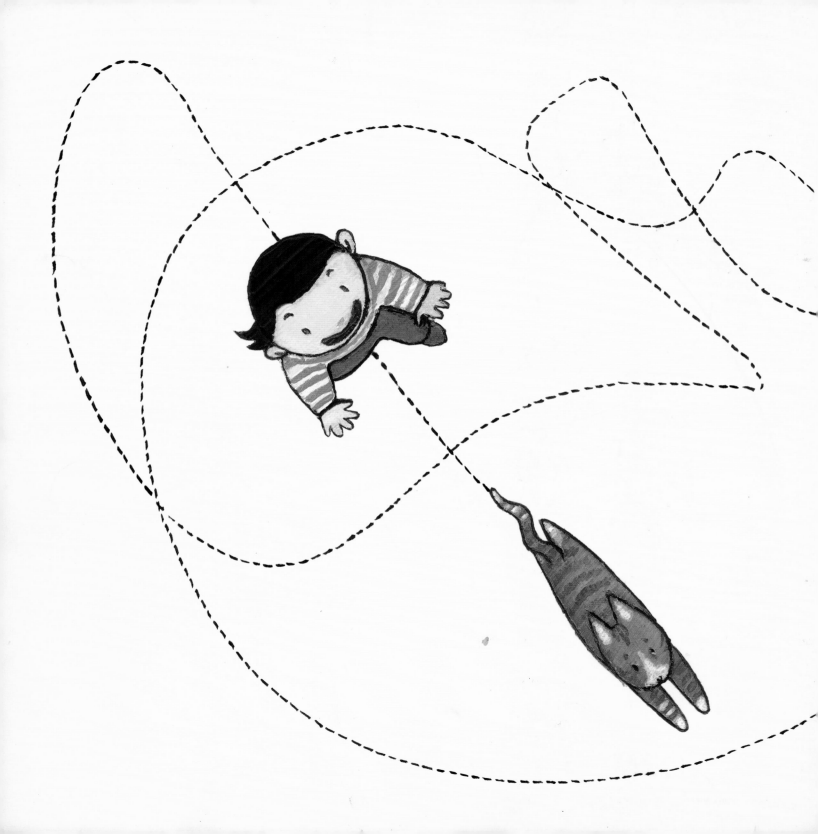